Dear Parent:

Congratulations! Your child is taking the first steps on an exciting journey. The destination? Independent reading!

STEP INTO READING® will help your child get there. The program offers five steps to reading success. Each story includes full-color art. There are also Step into Reading Sticker Readers, Step into Reading Write-In Readers, and Step into Reading Phonics, a complete literacy program with something for every child.

Learning to Read, Step by Step!

Ready to Read   Preschool–Kindergarten
• big type and easy words • rhyme and rhythm • picture clues
For children who know the alphabet and are eager to begin reading.

Reading with Help   Preschool–Grade 1
• basic vocabulary • short sentences • simple stories
For children who recognize familiar words and sound out new words with help.

Reading on Your Own   Grades 1–3
• engaging characters • easy-to-follow plots • popular topics
For children who are ready to read on their own.

Reading Paragraphs   Grades 2–3
• challenging vocabulary • short paragraphs • exciting stories
For newly independent readers who read simple sentences with confidence.

Ready for Chapters   Grades 2–4
• chapters • longer paragraphs • full-color art
For children who want to take the plunge into chapter books but still like colorful pictures.

STEP INTO READING® is designed to give every child a successful reading experience. The grade levels are only guides. Children can progress through the steps at their own speed, developing confidence in their reading, no matter what their grade.

Remember, a lifetime love of reading starts with a single step!

www.stepintoreading.com

www.randomhouse.com/kids/disney

Educators and librarians, for a variety of teaching tools, visit us at www.randomhouse.com/teachers

Library of Congress Cataloging-in-Publication Data
Jordan, Apple.
The big cheese / by Apple Jordan; illustrated by the Disney Storybook Artists.
p. cm. — (Step into reading. Step 2)
"Disney/Pixar Ratatouille."
ISBN 978-0-7364-2430-1 (trade)
ISBN 978-0-7364-8053-6 (lib. bdg.)
I. Disney Storybook Artists. II. Ratatouille (Motion picture) III. Title.
PZ7.J755Big 2007   2006037801

Printed in the United States of America 10 9 8

Disney · PIXAR
RATATOUILLE
(rat·a·too·ee)

The Big Cheese

By Apple Jordan

Illustrated by the Disney Storybook Artists

Random House New York

Remy was a rat.
His job was
to smell the garbage.
He made sure
it was safe to eat.
But Remy did not
like his job.

Remy was not
like other rats.
He did not
like garbage.

6

He liked good food.
He wanted
to be a chef.

One day,
Remy wanted to find
the perfect spice.

He crept into
a kitchen.

The old lady
who lived there
woke up.

She chased the rats.

But Remy did not leave.

He had to grab

a cookbook.

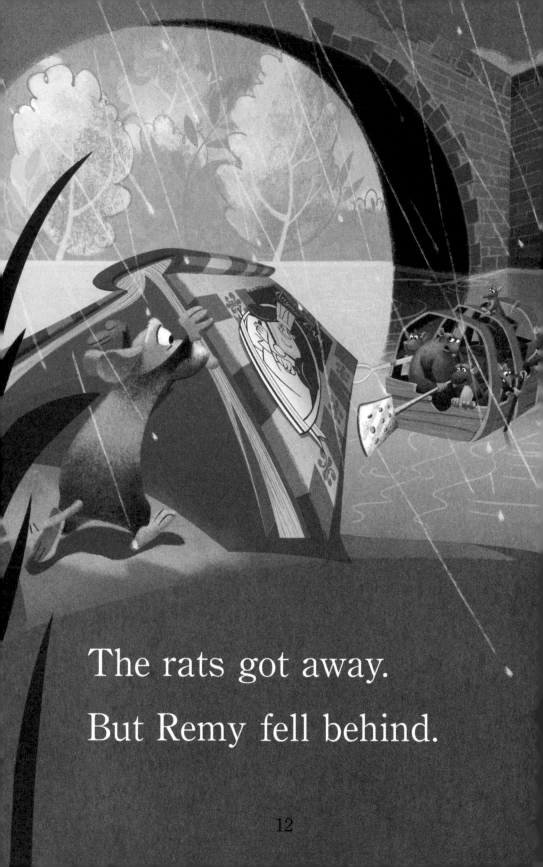

The rats got away.
But Remy fell behind.

Remy tried to catch up.

It was no use.

He was all alone.

Remy ended up
in Paris!
He saw
a fine restaurant!

Remy looked inside
the restaurant.
A boy named Linguini
tried to make soup.
Remy knew the soup
would be bad!

Remy fell into
the kitchen.
He had to get out!

But first
he fixed the soup.

The chef saw the rat.
He told Linguini
to get rid of Remy.

But Linguini knew that
Remy had made
his soup taste good.

He asked Remy
to help him cook.

Remy and Linguini
cooked together.

They were
a good team!

One day,
Remy found
his family.

They wanted Remy
to stay with them.
But Remy wanted
to stay with Linguini.

Everyone thought
Linguini was
a great chef.
But Remy was
the <u>real</u> chef!

Remy and Linguini
had a fight!
Linguini told Remy
to leave.

Then Ego,
the food critic,
came to the restaurant.

Remy knew he had
to help his friend.
He made
the best meal ever!

Ego asked to meet
the chef.

He was shocked.

The best chef in France
was a rat!

Soon Remy and Linguini
opened a restaurant.
The rats could eat
there, too!

Remy was happy.

He was a chef at last!